TIME WARP TRIO™

vol. 1

NIGHTMARE ON JOE'S STREET

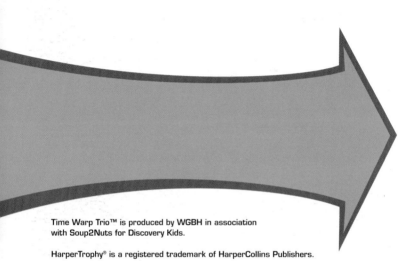

Time Warp Trio™ is produced by WGBH in association
with Soup2Nuts for Discovery Kids.

HarperTrophy® is a registered trademark of HarperCollins Publishers.

Time Warp Trio®
Time Warp Trio: Nightmare on Joe's Street
Copyright © 2006 WGBH Educational Foundation and Chucklebait, Inc.
Artwork, Designs and Animation © 2005 WGBH Educational Foundation.

For information address HarperCollins Children's Books,
a division of HarperCollins Publishers,
1350 Avenue of the Americas, New York, NY 10019.
www.harpercollinschildrens.com

Library of Congress catalog card number: 2006924548
ISBN-10: 0-06-111639-4—ISBN-13: 978-0-06-111639-1

Book design by Joe Merkel
❖
First HarperTrophy edition, 2006

TIME WARP TRIO

vol. **1**

NIGHTMARE ON JOE'S STREET

CREATED BY
JON SCIESZKA

ADAPTED BY
ZACHARY RAU

ADAPTED FROM THE
TELEPLAY BY
PETER K. HIRSCH

■ HarperTrophy®
An Imprint of HarperCollinsPublishers

TIME WARP TRIO CHARACTERS

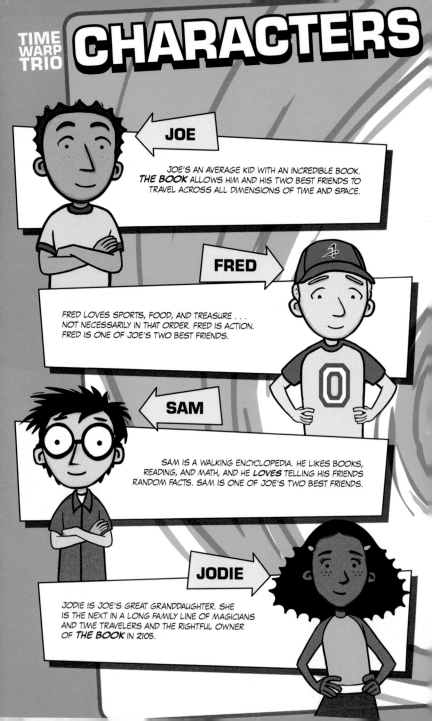

JOE

JOE'S AN AVERAGE KID WITH AN INCREDIBLE BOOK. *THE BOOK* ALLOWS HIM AND HIS TWO BEST FRIENDS TO TRAVEL ACROSS ALL DIMENSIONS OF TIME AND SPACE.

FRED

FRED LOVES SPORTS, FOOD, AND TREASURE . . . NOT NECESSARILY IN THAT ORDER. FRED IS ACTION. FRED IS ONE OF JOE'S TWO BEST FRIENDS.

SAM

SAM IS A WALKING ENCYCLOPEDIA. HE LIKES BOOKS, READING, AND MATH, AND HE *LOVES* TELLING HIS FRIENDS RANDOM FACTS. SAM IS ONE OF JOE'S TWO BEST FRIENDS.

JODIE

JODIE IS JOE'S GREAT GRANDDAUGHTER. SHE IS THE NEXT IN A LONG FAMILY LINE OF MAGICIANS AND TIME TRAVELERS AND THE RIGHTFUL OWNER OF *THE BOOK* IN 2105.

MARY SHELLEY AND PERCY BYSSHE SHELLEY

MARY SHELLEY LIVED FROM 1797 TO 1851. DURING THE SUMMER OF 1816, MARY AND HER HUSBAND, POET PERCY BYSSHE SHELLEY, LEFT ENGLAND TO STAY AT LORD BYRON'S HOUSE IN SWITZERLAND, WHERE MARY FOUND INSPIRATION FOR HER MOST FAMOUS BOOK, *FRANKENSTEIN*.

LORD BYRON

LIVED BETWEEN 1788–1824. HE WAS A FAMOUS POET WHO REBELLED AGAINST CONSERVATIVE POLITICS AND VALUES. HE FOUND ENGLAND TOO CONVENTIONAL FOR HIS TASTE, SO HE MOVED TO SWITZERLAND IN 1816. HE HOSTED MARY SHELLEY AND HER HUSBAND AT HIS HOUSE ON LAKE GENEVA ONE SUMMER.

THE MONSTER

THIS FICTIONAL CHARACTER WANTS TO FIND THE WOMAN WHO CREATED HIM, MARY SHELLEY. THEN MAYBE HE'LL KNOW WHY SHE MADE HIM SUCH AN UGLY BEAST. HE HAS A HOT TEMPER, ENJOYS A WIDE VARIETY OF MUSIC, AND LOVES TO EAT METAL OBJECTS.

THE BOOK

JOE RECEIVED *THE BOOK* AS A BIRTHDAY PRESENT FROM HIS UNCLE JOE. IT CAN WARP ANYONE TO ANY TIME AND ANY PLACE IN HISTORY. WHILE THAT SOUNDS REALLY COOL, THERE'S ONE PROBLEM: THE ONLY WAY TO GET BACK TO WHERE YOU CAME FROM IS TO FIND *THE BOOK* IN THE TIME AND PLACE YOU WARPED INTO. AND WHENEVER *THE BOOK* IS USED FOR TIME TRAVEL, IT HAS A HABIT OF DISAPPEARING.

AT JOE'S HOUSE IN BROOKLYN, NY . . .

Yawn!

OH, NO!

WHAT WAS *THAT*?

JUST THE WIND.

SCHUYLER, I'M *SERIOUS!* I HEARD SOMETHING IN THE FRONT HALL!

ALL RIGHT, TARA. I'LL CHECK IT OUT!

NO! THE PIGMAN IS IN THERE!

13

WHERE IS THIS MARY SHELLEY?

I MUST FIND HER!

THE MONSTER GOES ON A RAMPAGE LOOKING FOR MARY SHELLEY AND DESTROYS JOE'S HOUSE!

GRRRRRRR!

CRASH!

WHOA!

WAIT! YOU'RE NOT GOING TO FIND HER HERE.

Smash!

BANG!

YOU'RE NOT GOING TO FIND HER ANYWHERE. SHE LIVED IN THE NINETEENTH CENTURY.

HEY, I FOUND A PAGE ABOUT MARY SHEL—

♪♪ I'M A LITTLE TEAPOT, SHORT AND STOUT. HERE IS MY HANDLE, HERE IS MY SPOUT . . . ♪

PRETTY SOUNDS!

IT CALMED HIM DOWN. I GUESS MUSIC REALLY DOES SOOTHE THE SAVAGE BEAST.

JOE ACTIVATES *THE BOOK* . . .

I'M A YANKEE DOODLE DANDY . . .

. . . WHICH WARPS THE BOYS AND THE MONSTER . . .

JOE WARPED THEM BACK IN TIME AS QUICKLY AS HE COULD, BUT LOST SOMETHING IMPORTANT IN THE PROCESS.

HEY, AT LEAST I GOT US TO THE RIGHT PLACE. THIS LOOKS JUST LIKE—

UH, OH . . .

OH GREAT. SO NOW WE HAVE TO FIND MARY SHELLEY *AND THE BOOK.*

I *KNEW* THIS WAS A BAD IDEA.

WELL, WHAT WERE WE *SUPPOSED* TO DO?

CALL THE POLICE AND TELL THEM A FICTIONAL MONSTER WAS TRASHING MY KITCHEN AND MAKING YOU SING NURSERY RHYMES?

JUST THEN, THE MONSTER GRABS JOE . . .

Yoink!

WHAT IS THIS PLACE?

SWITZERLAND, 1816 . . . I HOPE!

AND MY CREATOR IS HERE?

MARY SHELLEY SPENT A SUMMER VACATIONING HERE WITH HER HUSBAND, THE POET PERCY BYSSHE SHELLEY.

NOW, IF ONLY WE COULD FIND OUT WHERE EXACTLY—

HEY, WE'LL ASK THEM!

ARE YOU CRAZY? THEY'LL TAKE ONE LOOK AT HIM AND BE OFF IN A FLASH.

Hmmmmm ...

YOU'RE RIGHT.

YOU'RE GOING TO HAVE TO HIDE WHILE WE FIND YOUR CREATOR.

NO! YOU WILL BRING ME TO HER!

BUT WE'LL NEVER GET TO HER IF YOU COME WITH US. YOU'LL SCARE EVERYONE AWAY!

FINE. BUT IF YOU DO NOT RETURN WITH THIS MARY SHELLEY, I WILL WREAK MY VENGEANCE . . .

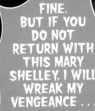

. . . ON HIM!

YOINK!

26

JOE, YOU SHOULD NOT BE OUT. NIGHT WILL BE UPON US SOON AND THESE WOODS ARE FILLED WITH CREATURES, WILD AND STRANGE.

YOU DON'T KNOW THE HALF OF IT.

MR. BYRON, YOU WOULDN'T HAPPEN TO KNOW A WOMAN NAMED MARY SHELLEY, WOULD YOU?

YOU'RE WITH MARY AND PERCY!

I SHOULD HAVE GUESSED—

ALL THEIR FRIENDS DRESS SO STRANGELY.

HOP IN! THEY'RE AT MY VILLA.

TO JOE'S SURPRISE, HE'S GREETED BY A FAMILIAR FACE.

GASP!

YOU?

OH!

WHAT ARE *YOU* DOING HERE? ARE YOU . . . LOST?

Ha ha ha!

I LOVE IT!

I AM *NOT* LOST!

I WAS GOING TO EGYPT IN 44 B.C.E.

I JUST MISSED MY WARP-TARGET, THAT'S ALL.

YEAH, WELL, ONE OF THOSE STORIES HAS COME TRUE. THE MONSTER FROM MARY'S BOOK SHOWED UP IN MY HALL CLOSET.

THAT'S IMPOSSIBLE! SHE WON'T EVEN WRITE *FRANKENSTEIN* FOR ANOTHER YEAR.

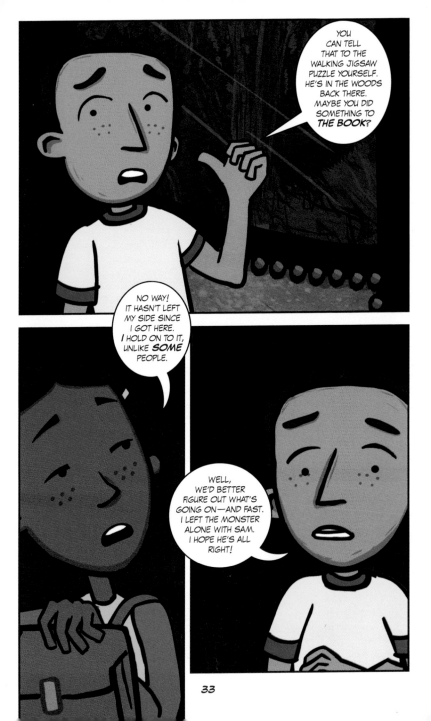

33

DID YOU KNOW THAT **MARY SHELLEY** WAS ONLY 19 YEARS OLD WHEN SHE WROTE **FRANKENSTEIN?** ALONG WITH HER HUSBAND, **PERCY BYSSHE SHELLEY** (A WORLD-RENOWNED ROMANTIC POET), SHE VACATIONED IN SWITZERLAND DURING THE "**YEAR WITHOUT A SUMMER.**" (A VOLCANO ERUPTION THE YEAR BEFORE HAD FILLED THE EARTH'S ATMOSPHERE WITH ASH, CREATING A COLD SUMMER.)

MARY SHELLEY
AUTHOR

DRAMATIZATION DRAMATIZATION DRAMATIZATION DRAMATIZATION

STUCK INSIDE, THE GUESTS AGREED TO **LORD BYRON'S** REQUEST OF TELLING GHOST STORIES AT NIGHT. MARY GOT THE IDEA FOR **FRANKENSTEIN** AFTER A NIGHTMARE SHE HAD.

DREAM-CAM

IN OTHER NEWS . . .

SOURCES SAY THAT IT WAS **LORD BYRON** WHO INSPIRED HIS PHYSICIAN AND HOUSEGUEST, **DR. POLIDORI**, TO WRITE **THE VAMPYRE**. DR. POLIDORI'S BOOK (WHICH WAS PUBLISHED IN 1819) WAS THE FIRST TIME THE "MODERN" VAMPIRE SHOWED UP IN LITERATURE.

LORD BYRON
HOST / VAMPIRE?

THESE TWO TALES HAVE BEEN SCARING READERS SINCE THE **NINETEENTH CENTURY!**

AND NOW . . . BACK TO OUR STORY . . .

I HAVE SOMETHING YOU'LL LIKE. I JUST REMEMBERED!

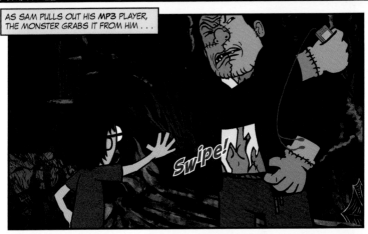

AS SAM PULLS OUT HIS **MP3** PLAYER, THE MONSTER GRABS IT FROM HIM . . .

Swipe!

. . . AND TRIES TO EAT IT!

YUM! YUM!

NO, NOT FOOD.

MUSIC. BEAUTIFUL MUSIC!

40

43

AT VILLA DIODATI, THE HOME OF LORD BYRON . . .

. . . DR. POLIDORI RECITES HIS NEWEST POEM.

THEY HASTENED, WITH RAPIDITY, TO PROTECT THE INNOCENT MAIDEN . . .

. . . BUT, ALAS, SHE WAS NO MORE! THE SWEET CHILD'S VERMILLION LIFE-LIQUID HAD BEEN DRAINED . . .

HOW MUCH MORE OF THIS DO WE HAVE TO LISTEN TO?

I'M WORRIED ABOUT SAM.

46

I'M AFRAID PERCY'S RIGHT. PERHAPS YOU SHOULD TRY CHANGING THE VAMPIRE FROM A ONE-LEGGED FISHMONGER NAMED BIGGLES TO SOMEONE A BIT MORE HANDSOME AND WICKED. SOMEONE LIKE . . .

WELL, LIKE OUR LORD BYRON HERE!

HE'D MAKE AN *EXCELLENT* VAMPIRE!

I HAVE A BETTER SUGGESTION.

STICK TO MEDICINE AND GIVE UP WRITING ALTOGETHER.

WHO WANTS TO GO NEXT?

MARY, DO YOU HAVE ANYTHING YET?

NO.

BUT I DID HAVE THE MOST HORRIBLE VISION LAST NIGHT. I SUPPOSE IT COULD BE TURNED INTO A STORY. HERE, I'LL READ IT TO YOU.

MARY SHELLEY FISHES AROUND IN HER BAG; SHE'S LOOKING FOR HER NOTEBOOK . . .

OH, DEAR! THIS ISN'T MY NOTEBOOK.

THE BOOK!

Oh!

Gasp!

HOW DID YOU GET THAT?

I HAVEN'T THE SLIGHTEST.

OH, WAIT. I REMEMBER! YOU LEFT YOUR BAG IN MY ROOM THE OTHER NIGHT.

WHEN I AWOKE FROM MY NIGHTMARE, I COULDN'T FIND MY NOTEBOOK.

THEN I SAW YOURS PEEKING OUT FROM THE BAG.

Scribble! Scribble!

I DIDN'T WANT TO LOSE THE IMAGE, SO I SCRIBBLED IT DOWN IN THE MARGIN OF A PAGE.

Scritch! Scritch!

I MUST HAVE FORGOTTEN TO PUT IT BACK IN YOUR BAG. I'M TERRIBLY SORRY.

53

TERRIFIED, PERCY FAINTS.

WANT TO KNOW HOW THIS MONSTROUS-LOOKING CREATURE CAME TO BE? **MARY SHELLEY** PUBLISHED HER NOVEL **FRANKENSTEIN** IN 1819. IT FOLLOWS **DR. VICTOR FRANKENSTEIN** AS HE TRIES TO BRING A DEAD BODY BACK TO LIFE. BUT AS SOON AS HE SEES HIS GHOULISH CREATION UP AND ABOUT, HE FREAKS OUT AND RUNS AWAY. I BET YOU WOULD DO THE SAME!

FILE FOOTAGE

FRANKENSTEIN'S MONSTER
FICTIONAL CREATURE

IN THE STORY, THE MONSTER LEAVES THE HOUSE TO EXPLORE THE WORLD ON HIS OWN. HE STARTS OUT BEING VERY KIND. HE ONLY WANTS FRIENDS. BUT PEOPLE'S REACTION TO HIM MADE HIM VIOLENT.

FORTUNATELY, THERE WAS SOMETHING THAT COULD CALM *THE MONSTER* . . .

HE LOVED GENTLE, SOOTHING MUSIC.

REMEMBER *THAT* THE NEXT TIME YOU COME FACE-TO-FACE WITH A *TEN-FOOT-TALL MONSTER!*

AND NOW BACK TO OUR STORY, ALREADY IN PROGRESS . . .

. . . SO YOU SEE, IT'S NOT JUST A TIME-TRAVELING DEVICE. IT IS ACTUALLY THE WHOLE SPACE-TIME CONTINUUM!

UH, YEAH, I GUESS. ACTUALLY, I DIDN'T KNOW ABOUT THAT PART BEFORE.

AND THIS MAGIC BOOK CAN TURN FICTIONAL CHARACTERS INTO LIVING PEOPLE?

I MUST HAVE IT. NAME YOUR PRICE!

SORRY, IT'S NOT FOR SALE.

WELL, FOR STARTERS, I WOULDN'T LEAVE MY BEST FRIEND ALONE WITH A TEN-FOOT-TALL, ANGRY, WALKING DEAD GUY.

SAM, YOU'RE ALIVE! HOW DID YOU FIND US?

EASY. I FOLLOWED THE TRAIL OF BROKEN TREES THE MONSTER LEFT BEHIND.

THAT GUY'S GOING TO DEFOREST SWITZERLAND UNLESS WE STOP HIM.

I'M COMING, TOO. IF WHAT YOU SAY IS TRUE, THEN I'M THE ONE HE WANTS.

MARY, YOU MUSTN'T! IT'S TOO DANGEROUS FOR A LADY!

A WOMAN CAN FACE A MONSTER JUST AS WELL AS A MAN, YOUR LORDSHIP.

ESPECIALLY, WHEN IT IS OF HER OWN CREATION.

ALL RIGHT. BUT ALLOW ME TO JOIN YOU. THERE IS SAFETY IN NUMBERS.

ARE YOU COMING, POLIDORI?

ER, I WOULD, BUT . . . SOMEONE MUST ATTEND TO POOR PERCY!

FINE!

POLIDORI GETS AN IDEA . . .

Heh!

Heh!

Heh!

ROOOOAAAAAAR!

MEANWHILE, THE MONSTER CONTINUES TO WREAK HAVOC.

WOULD YOU *PLEASE* STOP ROARING? MY EARS ARE *KILLING* ME!

IF YOU DO NOT LIKE MY VOICE . . .

. . . YOU SHOULD HAVE CREATED ME WITH A PRETTIER ONE!

70

WHY?

BECAUSE I'M HIDEOUS, THAT'S WHY!

OKAY, OKAY! I ADMIT IT.

YOU'RE HIDEOUS. BUT I CAN HELP YOU.

HOW?

THEY COULD BE ANYWHERE BY NOW. YOU SHOULD SEE HOW FAST HE CAN RUN.

YES, THAT'S HOW I IMAGINED HIM. PHYSICALLY, MORE POWERFUL THAN ANY MAN, AND DRIVEN BY AN UNRELENTING THIRST FOR REVENGE.

TOO BAD YOU DIDN'T IMAGINE HIM WITH A HEAD THAT GLOWS IN THE DARK. IT'D BE EASIER TO FIND THEM.

THAT SOUNDS LIKE ONE OF POLIDORI'S IDEAS. I WONDER WHAT THAT SCREEVING MUMPER IS UP TO?

74

BACK AT LORD BYRON'S VILLA, THE SCREEVING MUMPER WAS PLAYING WITH A POWER HE DIDN'T UNDERSTAND. HE HAD *THE BOOK*.

WHAT CANNOT BE BOUGHT–

CAN ALWAYS BE STOLEN.

CHARACTERS DON'T LEAP OFF THE PAGE, EH? WE'LL SEE ABOUT THAT.

DR. POLIDORI STARTED WRITING.

Scribble!

Scribble!

Scribble!

Scribble!

"IN HIS TWENTY-EIGHTH YEAR, LORD BYRON, AUTHOR OF THE POEM 'CHILDE HAROLD,' UNDERWENT A MYSTERIOUS CHANGE . . ."

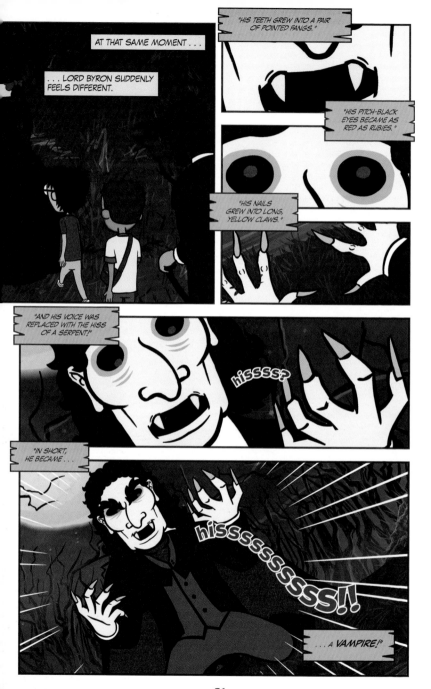

QUICKLY! INTO THE CASTLE! THERE ARE LOTS OF PLACES TO HIDE.

Huff!

Huff!

Pant!

Pant!

AS JOE, SAM, AND MARY RUN INTO THE CASTLE, JODIE IS PUTTING THE FINISHING TOUCHES ON HER MASTERPIECE.

WELL, I GUESS THAT'LL HAVE TO DO. I'M ALL OUT OF BASE.

YOUR EXTREME MONSTER MAKEOVER IS FINISHED.

I'D SHOW YOU WHAT YOU LOOK LIKE, BUT YOU ATE MY MIRROR.

OOOOOOH, CRUNCHY!

79

WARM. SWEET. NICE.

GRRRR! FRIENDS! LET ME HUG YOU!

Eeeeewww!

WHAT **HAPPENED** TO HIM?

THAT'S NOT THE REACTION WE WERE HOPING FOR. MAYBE YOU SHOULD BE A LITTLE MORE POSITIVE!

UMM . . .

NICE COAT?

SWIPE!

NO MORE GAMES!

OF COURSE, I HAVE **THE BOOK** . . .

. . . OF LOVE POETRY?

Poèmes d'Amore

NICE ONE, GRAMPS!

W-WELL . . . GUYS?

WHICH IS IT GOING TO BE?

THE BOYS PLAY MONSTER BAIT . . .

Thump!

Thump!

Thump!

NOW! *RUN!*

. . . AND BEGIN TO LEAD THE MONSTER AROUND THE TOWER OF THE CASTLE.

THEN THE GIRLS CONFRONT THE VAMPIRE . . .

BITE ME, SNAGGLETOOTH!

PPPPBBBBBBBTTTTT!!

. . . AND LEAD HIM TO THE MONSTER.

THE MONSTER AND BYRON FIGHT THEIR WAY ACROSS THE TOWER, UNTIL THE MONSTER TRIPS ON THE CASTLE'S LOW WALL AND . . .

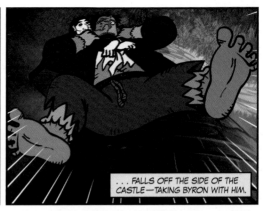

. . . FALLS OFF THE SIDE OF THE CASTLE—TAKING BYRON WITH HIM.

GASP!

GULP!

DO YOU THINK THEY'LL SURVIVE?

I DON'T KNOW ABOUT THE MONSTER. I NEVER IMAGINED HIM IN WATER.

BUT BYRON MIGHT LIVE. HE'S AN EXCELLENT SWIMMER.

WHAT HAPPENED TO HIM ANYWAY? ONE MINUTE HE WAS AN ECCENTRIC POET . . .

. . . THE NEXT, HE WAS AN ECCENTRIC POET WITH FANGS.

I HAVE A PRETTY GOOD IDEA.

C'MON. LET'S GET BACK TO THE VILLA BEFORE THE MUMMY AND THE WEREWOLF SHOW UP.

THE COMMOTION FINALLY WAKES PERCY.

OH, MARY. I HAD THE MOST *TERRIBLE* DREAM!

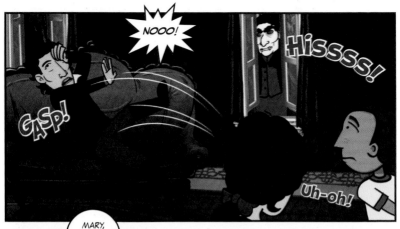

NOOO!

HISSSS!

GASP!

Uh-oh!

MARY, YOU WERE RIGHT.

BYRON **IS** AN EXCELLENT SWIMMER.

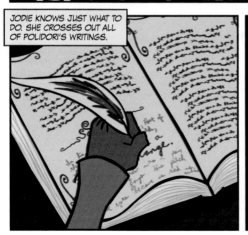

JODIE KNOWS JUST WHAT TO DO. SHE CROSSES OUT ALL OF POLIDORI'S WRITINGS.

AS SHE DOES, EVERYTHING RETURNS TO NORMAL . . .

YOU'RE *NOT* GOING TO WRITE *FRANKENSTEIN?*

BUT YOU *HAVE* TO.

IT'S A CLASSIC. IT'S THE GRANDFATHER OF ALL HORROR FICTION!

AND THE GRANDMOTHER OF GREAT HALLOWEEN COSTUMES!

I'M SORRY, BUT HAVING ACTUALLY SEEN THE MONSTER THAT LURKED IN MY MIND, I JUST CAN'T BRING HIM TO LIFE . . . IN *ANY* FORM.

IN FACT, I'VE DECIDED TO GIVE UP WRITING ALTOGETHER. IT'S TOO DANGEROUS.

THANK YOU ALL SO MUCH FOR SHOWING ME THE ERROR OF MY WAYS.

THE TIME-WARPERS TRAVEL BACK IN TIME TO THE NIGHT MARY SHELLEY HAD HER DREAM.

GOOD. SHE'S STILL ASLEEP.

AND THERE'S *THE BOOK*– RIGHT WHERE I LEFT IT.

THINK YOU CAN HOLD ON TO IT THIS TIME?

JUST TRY TO FIND MARY'S NOTEBOOK WITHOUT WAKING HER UP!

I FOUND IT!

Plunk!

FWOOOSH!

DON'T MOVE A MUSCLE.

BEFORE MARY GETS A SECOND LOOK AT JOE, THE BOYS ARE GONE.

HUH?

Scribble! Scribble! Scribble! Scribble!

WE'RE BACK. NO MORE VAMPIRES, NO MORE MONSTERS.

YEAH, JUST A KITCHEN THAT'S GOING TO TAKE **HOURS** TO CLEAN.

HEY! DO YOU HEAR SOMETHING?

NO . . .

NEITHER DID I.

THE RAIN HAS STOPPED!

C'MON, LET'S GET SOME PIZZA. WE'RE GOING TO NEED SOME FUEL FOR THE LONG NIGHT AHEAD.

HEY, REMEMBER THE PART WHERE THE VAMPIRE AND THE MONSTER WERE BATTLING IT OUT IN THE CASTLE?

THAT WAS SO **COOL!**

COOL???

WE ALMOST DIED! WHAT'S COOL ABOUT THAT?

THE ALMOST PART.

THE END